GLORY RETURNS

Wayne Reed

Bloomington, IN — authorHOUSE — Milton Keynes, UK

AuthorHouse™
1663 Liberty Drive, Suite 200
Bloomington, IN 47403
www.authorhouse.com
Phone: 1-800-839-8640

AuthorHouse™ UK Ltd.
500 Avebury Boulevard
Central Milton Keynes, MK9 2BE
www.authorhouse.co.uk
Phone: 08001974150

This book is a work of fiction. People, places, events, and situations are the product of the author's imagination. Any resemblance to actual persons, living or dead, or historical events, is purely coincidental.

© 2006 Wayne Reed. All rights reserved.

No part of this book may be reproduced, stored in a retrieval system, or transmitted by any means without the written permission of the author.

First published by AuthorHouse 4/14/2006

ISBN: 1-4259-2635-5 (sc)

Library of Congress Control Number: 2006902361

Printed in the United States of America
Bloomington, Indiana

This book is printed on acid-free paper.

This work is dedicated
In loving memory
of my mother

Martha Palmer Reed

1919-2005

Forward

This is a work of fiction and any resemblance to real people, events, or plots is not the intent of this story. The events, people and plots of this work are creations of my mind. There is some truth in the pages of this story and this truth is why pen and ink have been put to paper. There is an Ark of the Covenant and it did lead Israel during the time they were wandering in the wilderness, it was the place God communicated with Moses, and it played a huge part in the daily lives of the people of Israel. Ethiopia openly claims the Ark of the Covenant is in the Chapel of St. Mary's in Aksum, Ethiopia and The Queen of Sheba did visit King Solomon. In other words most of the historical parts of this story are based on facts. The reference to the places and events described in country of Ethiopia can be found or seen by a study of the Ethiopian history and legend. I have found these facts to be most interesting and applied this interest to the pages of my story. Please read this story for enjoyment, as a fast fun read and not as a history book or a reference to events of today.

Accounts of the Ark of the Covenant are found in the same books, chapters, and verses in both the Old and New Testaments of the Christian Holy Bible and the Jewish Scriptures: The Torah (The Five Books of Moses}, The Nevi'im (The Prophets), and The Kethuvim (The Writings).

Glory Returns

The Beginning

Chapter 1

It would be a huge gathering because all the family was coming, and for the first time in months, there would be plenty of food. Aunts, uncles, and cousins had been arriving all day bringing covered dishes containing good smelling delights, and it was all happening to honor Ali. There had never been this much food in the home before and the aroma was causing his mouth to water. His younger brothers and sisters were enjoying the event almost as much as he was. It had been nearly a year since they all had gotten together for a celebration such as this one, only earlier that gathering had been for his brother Hassan. It made him feel important when he was embraced by the old women or patted on the back by the men. He was going to become someone important and they would all remember and celebrate him as a national hero for many years to come.

He had seen the pride on his father's face as everyone commented on the bravery of his sons and what great honor they brought to the family. Yes, it would be true; when this night was over, he would be a great hero forever, just as everyone had said.

There had been sadness in his mother's eyes; he had seen it just before the time came for him to start. He had seen this sadness in her eyes before. It had been there last year when the time arrived for his older brother to make his delivery. His brother's celebration had also been a special event for the family and his brother is still being honored as a great hero. Ali could still remember how proud he was of his older brother and how much he wanted to be like him. The people in the neighborhood often spoke of how brave and heroic his brother had been. Ali wanted so much to be like his older brother---and he would be just like him very soon.

"Ali," Hassan had said, "I can hardly contain my joy. Soon I'll be in paradise with any number of virgins to serve me."

"It does sound great," Ali had replied with pride in his heart for his brother, as well as with a bit of jealousy. "And what an honor it will be for our family to give a martyr to Allah for the jihad."

Ali thought about the hardships his family had experienced before his brother delivered his package and the check for twenty-five thousand dollars had come. The money had paid off the family debt, purchased the small house in which they now lived. It had also provided his younger brothers and sisters with new clothes, and enough food for his entire family. He was sure another check would arrive shortly after his delivery was completed and would once again make life easier for his family. He hoped after all the bills were paid, there would be enough for a washing machine for his mother and maybe a used car for his father. Mother had washed the family clothes by hand and father walked several miles each day to find work. He hoped his heroic action would make life easier for the family, as the General promised him it would.

They came for him just after the sun went down. Two of the General's most loyal men had been sent to accompany Ali to the secret location. He could feel the pride and excitement well up inside his chest as he left the family gathering to go pickup his package. He would be taken to the secret location to receive the package and then return to the party for his parting farewell.

The location of the building was one of the most protected secrets of the organization. The only ones to know the location of this building was the leaders, the few specialists that prepared the packages and the honored heroes that made the deliveries and they would never tell.

He had been told that two deliveries would be made this night and his childhood friend Karim would be making the other delivery. He hoped he would be able to talk with Karim at the secret building when he was picking up the other package. They talked earlier in the week and had made plans for the many happy days they would soon enjoy together and exchanged thoughts of what it would be like. Ali and Karim had always been close friends and now they were going to become honored heroes together.

"Who would have thought," Ali mused aloud to his friend, "that you and I both would have been selected for such an honor. No matter how hard our fathers work, there never seems to be quite enough money to put food on the table or clothes on our backs."

"I know," Karim agreed and added, 'but now this will change, and all for the better. You and I will be blessed martyrs in paradise, but also our families will have more food and goods than they have ever seen."

The secret building was on the edge of town and looked like all the others on the street. All the buildings in this part of town were old, run down, and in bad need of repair. The front of the building was a cluttered appliance repair shop, where two men were working on a cook stove. They did not often work this late in the evening and did not get much work done this night as they were always looking out at the street. Their purpose tonight was not to repair the cook stove but to be watchful for unwelcome guests that may come along. They kept their tool chest close by, for stored inside were automatic weapons, loaded and ready for trouble.

Ali was quickly escorted through the appliance shop to a small dark workroom in the back of the building. The only light was coming from two small desk lamps fastened to a low table where three men were working. They stopped their work and looked up as Ali entered the room. One of the men was heard saying quietly, "Allah be with you". On the table was a number of small bundles, rolls of wire, tape, and some hand tools. Each man was working cautiously on the special packages making sure each would make the delivery as planned.

Ali was disappointed to find Karim had already picked up his package and was on his way to make his delivery. He had hoped to see his friend one more time to arrange a meeting place in the meadow, but on second thought, it was all right that he had missed him now, because there would be plenty of time for them to be together. Ali could hardly control his emotions when he remembered what the general had told him about the many enjoyable things that awaited him. It was going to be only joy and happiness for him and Karim. He hoped his brother would be waiting for him as the General had promised.

"Just think," the General had smiled, his mouth opening to show white teeth---almost resembling a shark's--- slashed in a row within his black beard and moustache. "You, Ali, who have been poor and unknown, except within your family and your small group of friends, will soon be transported to paradise as a martyr to Islam and a hero for all of your people. How wonderful!"

"All I can think of now," Ali excitedly responded, "is to see my brother Hassan, meet my friend Karim, and the plans I have made for my virgins that are waiting for me."

Once inside the dark room, Ali was told to remove his jacket and shirt, and then he was fitted with the package. Smaller than he expected, fitting tightly around his waist and weighing about ten pounds, it was easy to conceal under his shirt. There were several colored wires extending from the package, one red wire had a small switch on the end of it. He was told to flip this switch and press the small button located in front of it when it was time to make the delivery. There was also a back-up pressure switch if someone tried to steal or remove the package before time came for him to make this very special delivery.

After the package was fitted, Ali was given his final instructions and told the details of where and how to complete the delivery. He was then driven back to his father's house and the celebration, where his picture was taken and he received the best wishes of the family and friends. Ali's picture would soon hang beside his brother's and everyone that saw it would know he was an honored hero just like his brother. Just the thought of being compared to his older brother caused him to stand a little taller and put a smile on his face. He felt as if his heart would burst with pride.

Chapter 2

He left the party and his family with great excitement, but well aware of the bulk and growing weight of the package wrapped around his waist. The packaged seemed to grow heavier as he kissed his Mother goodbye. The jacket he wore felt good as the coolness of the night crept upon him and he gave a slight shiver from the cold or was this just from the excitement of the of the coming events.

Ali had always been shy and did not have any experience with girls. In a few short hours this would all change and he would be running in a lush green meadow with many young virgins, who would be there just for his pleasure. He knew Karim had just left the party that was held in his honor and was making this same journey to deliver his special package. Ali was sure Karim was having the same expectations of the many virgins and what it would be like to be with them. His thoughts of the next few hours were so great he could hardly conceal his emotions as he waited at the corner bus stop.

As he climbed the steps he noticed there were not many people riding the bus at this time of night. Since there were many empty seats he was able to sit by himself. He could now relax some, because he had worried that someone sitting next to him might discover the special package he carried and he would not be able to deliver it at 9:55 as planned. The plan called for Karim and Ali to deliver both their special packages at precisely 9:55 PM. The ride to the disco club was not a long one and went by uneventfully and quickly.

Arriving at the disco club with time to spare, Ali worked his way into the crowd of young people all moving with the beat of the music. This was a busy night at the club and it was over crowded. A very popular local band was playing for the neighborhood and every teenager in the surrounding area was enjoying the entertainment. Ali noticed all the young couples laughing and dancing as the colored lights flashed with the beat of the music. One cute red haired girl about sixteen years old was smiling at him as he pushed his way past her. Ali had seen her working in her parents' bagel shop last week when he and Karim were walking in the market. Karim had said she had smiled at him and had given him the come- on-over- and- talk look, but being shy as he was he could not make himself go talk with her then.

He wanted to stop and talk with her now, but that would not be a wise thing to do on this special night. Besides, he had noticed the Star of David on the gold chain that hung around her neck. There was much more important business to attend to this night, and his virgins were going to be a lot more beautiful than this Jew-girl and they were all waiting just for him.

He looked at his watch and was growing more excited as the second hand moved closer to the 9:55 deadline. Ali slowly moved into the center of the room, and with five seconds remaining he slid his hand into his coat and found the switch and started to apply pressure. At exactly 9:55 PM, the blast ripped through his clothes and body, sending the package of screws and nails into the crowd. The blast had such force that the roof of the building was lifted up then came crashing down, crushing many of the youths already torn and bleeding from the many wounds caused by the bomb. Blood and body parts were splattered over everything and the cries of the dying could be heard coming from the rubble as the dust and smoke boiled out.

Chapter 3

Across town the meeting at the Temple had ended, and the Rabbi was saying good night to the last of the community leaders when a young man walked into the group of elderly men. It was exactly 9:55 PM` when Karim delivered his special package. The blast killed the Rabbi and six of the Elders. Many of the others would be rushed to the hospital, wounded and bleeding with the nails and screws embedded deeply in their body.

The total for the night had been twenty-four dead and thirty-two wounded, with two of these not expected to live through the night. One of the dead was a little girl about sixteen years old. There was a gold chain with the Star of David on it entangled in her blood- splattered red hair. Some of those wounded in the blast had been trapped in the rubble of the building and had burned to death screaming for help.

It had taken the police and fire departments most of the night to recover all of the injured and dead. The ambulance crews and medical staff worked throughout the night as victim after victim were brought into the emergency room. The halls were filled with the injured and dying as the staff raced to stop the bleeding and remove the pieces of metal from their bodies. This double attack had been the worst of the suicide bombings this year.

If their promise is kept Ali and Karim are now on their way to the arms of the seventy- two virgins that are waiting in the lush green meadow beside the cool flowing waters of the streams in paradise. Their mission had gone as planned with the special packages being delivered on time. The Palestinian leaders of Hamas were rejoicing in this latest successful operation. The General, as he likes to be called, is especially pleased with this latest operation. It had been the most successful of the forty-one special deliveries he had planned this year. The deliveries were always planned to take the largest number of casualties possible and most of them had done just that. A few special deliveries had been made earlier, when the hero and his package had been discovered. These few earlier deliveries had not produced the planned casualties, but that was all right, because the main purpose of the deliveries was not necessarily to kill or injure. It was to instill fear and show them that they could never live in peace on Palestinian land. They called him a terrorist, but to himself and his followers he is a true patriot and a soldier for Allah. This is a jihad, a religious war that he knew his side would win, for they had Allah on their side.

Chapter 4

The meeting started early with Prime Minister Benjamin holding up the morning newspapers. Below the headlines were the pictures of the dismembered bodies of the dead, and the bloodstains left by the wounded. The local newspapers always printed the pictures with the bloodiest victims, the dead, and the gore. Printing these pictures only helped spread the terror and caused more pain for the families of the victims. He wished he could control what pictures they printed, but he knew he could not.

He shouted to the men present, "God help me find a way to stop this insane murder of our people. Are we like sheep being led to the slaughter? Is there nothing we can do? We have already destroyed the General's home and office. Do we now send the tanks back in and kill them all or nuke the whole area and fry their asses?"

"The Americans would not like that," said Karl Greenburg, the Minister of Justice. "Sending in the tanks or frying their asses would only upset the Arabs worldwide and could cause us more problems."

"You are right, of course," replied the Prime Minster, "but something must be done. We cannot allow this insane attack on our people to continue."

"Where is our strength of old? Moses killed a task master for just beating a slave, but we just stand by and let this outrage exist." Zack Walker, Minster of Defense continued. "If only we had the wisdom of King Solomon we might find the solution to stop these attacks."

"Yes", replied Benjamin, "We were once a great nation. The world came to our feet bearing many gifts of treasure, seeking our friendship, and treaties. Israel of old was a world super power, proud people with great wealth and power. "Now we must suffer this insanity and rely on others for our safety." It's as if Israel has had a curse placed on it since the time of Solomon. These things have got to change; we must find a way to return our nation and our people to our former glory if we are ever to find peace."

One of the other Council Members spoke up saying, "There is a history professor from the USA, a black fellow, here doing some research into the power and greatness of Biblical Israel. I heard him talk at the University last week. He has come up with a theory that sounds far fetched, but he insists will return Israel to its former greatness. I met him again at the American Embassy last night; I believe his name is Doctor Markus Friedman."

Prime Minister Benjamin said, "If you believe this man has any information that will help us, then get him in here and let's hear what he has to say."

"Now let us decide how we are going to respond to these murderous attacks," said The Prime Minister.

After much discussion it was decided about all they could do was to send in the tanks and destroy some more Palestine buildings and surround the General's home and office. They could keep him and his people in house arrest and not let anyone in or out to plan more attacks. They could cut the telephone and electric lines to make life hard for those inside as a way to punish them. They wanted to kill the General, but to do so would only bring more trouble from all the Arabs, and the Americans would not be pleased. Prime Minster Benjamin did not like having to depend so heavily on the Americans for the protection of his country. But he was no fool, he knew without America's aid and protection Israel would not exist.

Zack asked with a chuckle, "Will we collect and return the bodies of these latest murders to the General the same way we have done with all the others?" "Yes we surely will", replied the Prime Minster with a slight smile on his face. 'We will collect all the body parts and after they have been prepared and processed they are to be sent back to the General. We must always show proper respect for the dead and give them the dignity that they deserve." The Prime Minster had given detailed instructions as to what must be done to prepare the bodies and exactly how they were to be returned.

Most of the people could not understand why they were being so generous by returning the bodies. What they did not know was the "process" used to prepare the bodies.

All of the body parts would be collected and carried down to a small windowless building close to the stockyards. There is a muddy pen connected to the back of this building that contained a herd of wild hogs. These pigs are fed very little until the time of processing the body of a suicide bomber. The bodies would be cut or torn into small pieces, all of the bones will be crushed, and then all of it will be given to the wild hogs as food. It's common knowledge that a hungry wild hog will eat almost anything. Once the bodies of the bombers have been processed through the intestines of the hogs the results will be collected and bagged. The bags will then be put on an aircraft that will drop the processed bodies on the roof of the General's headquarters. Their spirit maybe in a meadow with seventy-two virgins, but their bodies will be turned into pig manure.

The Prime Minster and all the cabinet members knew this "processing" of the bodies would be the most insulting thing they could do to one of these suicide bombers. To the believer of Islam a pig is considered an unclean animal. It would be a sin for them to eat pork, own swine, or even be in the presence of a pig.

Chapter 5

Dr. Markus, a professor of History at the University of Mississippi, is in Israel gathering information for his classes and looking for information that will prove his theory. He has spent the last three years researching the reasons for the greatness of Israel from the time of Moses to the kingdom of King Solomon. Markus is a small middle aged man who enjoys his work. He loves to research old manuscripts and visit sites where ancient events occurred. He does talk a lot and can at times be quite annoying. Most of his colleagues consider him to be a total nut with his constant research and theories. He is very much a loner, and during his three years being on staff at the University he has not made any friends.

What they had not known is that Dr. Markus's great grandfather had been a slave in the Mississippi Delta. Since his earliest childhood he had heard the old stories that had been passed down to his grandfather and father. It was told that as a very young child, his great grandfather had been taken from his mother and father and his homeland, Ethiopia and brought to America. Dr. Markus as a small child had sat and listened with careful interest as his grandfather told of the hardship suffer by everyone on the slave ship, about the many that died on the voyage, and how the bodies were cast into the sea.

His great grandfather had claimed his father's brother was a great King. The old stories also told of the history and relics of the great nation of their forefathers. The stories of great treasure that was buried around the great grandfather's home village of Aksum always put this mind to work thinking of this mysterious country.

The family name "Friedman" had been given to the young slave when it was discovered that he had been raised to worship God from the old books of the Hebrews. His family even now was the only black people in his area that worshiped a form of the Jewish religion.

Dr. Markus was in the museum searching through a pile of old Hebrew writings and manuscripts and did not see the four mountains moving toward him until a huge hand gripped his arm like a vise. The largest of the four spoke and said, "You will come with us" and he lifted Dr. Markus from his chair. When Dr. Markus started to object, one of the huge men showed him his identification badge and the semi-automatic pistol in his belt.

Dr. Markus was not a strong man and was visibly shaken from this unexpected encounter. Once placed in the black sedan, between two of the huge agents, he spoke softly in his southern accent, "What have I done? Tell me where are you taking me. I've done nothing wrong."

No one would look at him or answer his questions. Finally one of the giants said, "No harm will come to you, so just shut up and wait."

Nothing else was spoken until Dr. Markus was escorted into the office of the Defense Minster. Waiting for him was Zack Walker, Minster of Defense, and two other men that were unknown to Dr. Markus. Zack spoke first, "I'm sorry if we have disrupted your day but what we need from you pertains to Israel's national security."

Dr. Markus asked, "What do I know about your national security? I'm here as a guest in this country doing research for the college class I teach on the Jews of Biblical Times."

The Prime Minster, coming into the room behind Markus, spoke, "Dr. Markus, I am Prime Minster Benjamin; let me apologize for any inconvenience we must be causing you. I will assure you that no harm will come to you. May we offer you some coffee or tea?"

"No thanks," replied Dr. Markus, "but you can tell me why I've been brought here!"

"That's a fair question," said Prime Minster Benjamin. "We have asked you to come here to see if you can help us with a problem."

Markus was silent for a long minute then looked the Prime Minster in the eyes and said slowly, "What can "I" do to help you?"

The Prime Minster cleared his throat and began, "Are you aware of the carnage of last evening when two more suicide bomber struck our people?"

Markus moved his head up and down and said, "Yes, I saw the report on television this morning."

"We are trying to find a way to stop these attacks and are asking anyone with an idea to come forward and help us. It has been brought to our attention that you have a theory of what must be done to remove this curse and return Israel to its former glory."

Dr. Markus replied with a smile, "Most people think my theory is a little wacky. Are you sure you want to take the time to consider it?"

"Do you believe your theory will make Israel a great nation again?" asked the Prime Minister.

"Yes I do", replied Markus, "I'm sure of it."

"Then this is exactly what we want to discuss with you, your theory as to why our country suffers and what can be done to return it to greatness."

Markus' reply was not surprising to those that know of his willingness to give assistance when asked. "I would be happy tell you what my studies have uncovered, but first let me ask that you consider everything I show you before you accept or reject what I have discovered." I don't want you to discount what I have to say until you get the whole picture."

"That's fair enough," said the Prime Minster.

"What I'm about to relate to you is information I've uncovered and collected over the last three years as I have researched stories my grandfather told me when I was a young child. While searching for the truth in my grandfather's stories, I have discovered these untold facts. These untold facts are backed up from many sources, including the Old Testament Bible and the New Testament Christian Bible, the Torah, the Koran, The Dead Sea Scrolls, and many other ancient documents. You see, these documents have all been found to be historically and geographically correct; only the theological ideas differ. I will be referring to many of these documents as I relate my findings and my theory.

"Let's start with the Jews," Markus continued, "God's chosen people, who escaped slavery from Egypt and crossed the Red Sea. They camped at Mt. Sinai and Moses went up to the mountain and received instructions from God to build an Ark or chest in which to keep the tables of the law or The Ten Commandments, which God was about to give to Moses. I'm sure you all know this Bible story. The details for the construction of this chest are found in

Exodus 25: 10-22. It says, 'Have them make a chest of acacia wood—two and a half cubits long, a cubit and a half wide, and a cubit and a half high. Overlay it with pure gold, both inside and out, and make a molding of gold around it. Cast four feet, with two rings on one side and two on the other. Then make poles of acacia wood and overlay them with gold. Insert the poles into the rings on the sides of the chest to carry it. The poles are to remain in the rings of this ark. Then put in the ark the tables on which the law is written.

'Make an atonement cover of pure gold – two and a half cubits long and a cubit and a half wide. And make two cherubim out of hammered gold at the ends of the cover. Make one cherub on one end and the second on the other; make the cherubim of one piece with the cover, at the two ends. The cherubim are to have their wings spread upward, overshadowing the cover with them. The cherubim are to face each other and looking toward the cover. Place the cover on top of the ark and put in the Testimony, which I will give you. There, above the cover between the two cherubim that are over the ark of the testimony, I will meet with you and give you all my commands for the Israelites.'"

"What's a cubit?" asked Zack?

"It's a means of measurement, about 18 inches" said Dr. Markus. "The chest, which God had Moses build, is about 1.1 meter long and 0.7 meter wide and tall. The gold was brought out of Egypt with the people as they escaped slavery. The Egyptians had trained some of the former slaves as goldsmiths and they had made the fine gold jewelry and ornaments of the Pharaohs. So you see, there was an ample supply of gold and talent to build the Ark of the Covenant. "

Dr. Markus shifted in his seat, continuing aloud with his thoughts, as he would have if he had been in his classroom back in Oxford, Mississippi. "The Ark of the Covenant was an aid to the nation of Israel during the forty years they wandered in the wilderness. The Ark preceded the people by three days journey serving as a guide for Israel's campsites. Prayers accompanied each journeying and resting of the Ark: "Arise, O Lord, and let thy enemies be scattered... Return, O Lord, to the ten thousand thousands of Israel."

"Professor, are we here to hear a religious lesson from you or to hear how we can stop our enemies from killing our people?" asked the Defense Minister?

Dr. Markus replied, "Just bare with me a few more minutes and all will be revealed." Prime Minster Benjamin gave his Defense Minster a stern look.

Dr. Markus continued. "The Ark continued to play a huge part in the everyday lives of the Israelites. It is well recorded how Israel won battle after battle against incredible odds and it is written in Josh. 3 that the Ark cooperated at the crossing of the Jordan River.

The waters of the river ceased to flow as soon as the feet of the priests that were carrying the Ark entered the water. The river stood still above these priests until the people had crossed over and remained stilled until the priests left the bed of the river with the Ark. The Ark was also carried in the solemn march around the famed city of Jericho, which according to Josh. 6 caused the walls of the city to fall down.

"What I'm telling you," said Dr. Markus, "is that everything I have found affirms evidence that when the Ark of the Covenant is in the camp of Israel there is protection and good fortune for God's chosen people. The Lord time and again intervened mightily in Israel's behalf and gave victory over their enemies.

"My theory is further supported by evidence of defeats and troubles faced by Israel when the Ark of the Covenant was not in their possession. Bear with me as I read from the Old Testament Bible, 1 Samuel starting with chapter 4; this will help you understand." Dr. Markus dug into his old leather briefcase and pulled out a badly worn Bible. He opened it, turned to the desired page, and began to read aloud:

"'Now the Israelites went out to fight against the Philistines. The Israelites camped at Ebenezer, and the Philistines at Aphek. The Philistines deployed their forces to meet Israel, and as the battle spread, Israel was defeated by the Philistines, who killed about four thousand of them on the battlefield. When the soldiers returned to camp, the elders of Israel asked, "Why did the Lord bring defeat upon us today before the Philistines? Let us bring the Ark of the Lord's covenant from Shiloh, and they brought back the Ark of the Covenant of the Lord Almighty, who is enthroned between the cherubim.'

'When the ark of the Lord's covenant came into the camp, all Israel raised such a great shout that the ground shook. Hearing the uproar, the Philistines asked, "What's all the shouting in the Hebrew camp?"

'When they learned that the ark of the Lord had come into the camp, the Philistines were afraid. "A god has come into the camp," they said. "We're in trouble! Nothing like this has happened before. Woe to us! Who will deliver us from the hand of these mighty gods? They are the gods who struck the Egyptians with all kinds of plagues. Be strong, Philistines! Be men, or you will be subject to the Hebrews, as they have been to you. Be men, and fight!"

'So the Philistines fought, and the Israelites were defeated and every man fled to his tent. The slaughter was great; Israel lost thirty-thousand soldiers. The Ark of God was captured....The Glory has departed from Israel—for the ark of God has been captured.'".

Zack Walker interrupted asking, "If the Ark was in their camp, why was the Army of Israel defeated?"

Dr. Markus replied, "If you read some of the first chapters of 1 Samuel you will find that God was not always present with the Ark and God was not with Israel in this battle. It's as if they went into this battle without God's approval or they went in alone. Now let me read a little more and you will see what happened to the Philistines when they took the ark of God into their cities.

"In 1 Samuel 5, beginning with verse 1 it reads as follows: 'After the Philistines had captured the ark of God, they took it from Ebenezer to Ashdod.' Now skipping to verse 6, 'The lord's hand was heavy upon the people of Ashdod and its vicinity; he brought devastation upon them and afflicted them with tumors. When the men of Ashdod saw what was happening they said, "The ark of the god of Israel must not stay here with us, because his hand is heavy upon us and upon our god." So they called together all the rulers of the Philistines and asked them, "What shall we do with the ark of the god of Israel?" They answered, "Have the ark of the god of Israel moved to Gath." So they moved the ark of the god of Israel.

"But after they moved it, the Lord's hand was heavy against that city, throwing it into a great panic. He afflicted the people of the city, both young and old, with an outbreak of tumors. So they sent the ark of God to Ekron.

"As the Ark of God was entering Ekron, the people of Ekron cried out, 'They have brought the ark of the god of Israel around to us to kill us and our people.' So they called together all the rulers of the Philistines and said, 'Send the ark of the god of Israel away; let it go back to its own place, or it will kill us and our people.' For death had filled the city with panic; God's hand was very heavy upon it. Those who did not die were afflicted with tumors, and the outcry of the city went up to heaven.

"When the ark of the Lord had been in Philistine territory seven months, the Philistines called for the priests and the diviners and said, 'What shall we do with the ark of the Lord? Tell us how we should send it back.'"

Laying the Bible down, Dr Markus looked up and said, "The Philistines took the Ark into their cities as a trophy of the victory over the Israelites. Soon after the Ark entered the city, the Philistines begin to experience many unexplained calamities. Large painful cancerous tumors started appearing on the people causing many of them to die. Tumors, death and many other terrible problems continued to come upon the Philistines as the Ark remained in their possession and was moved from city to city. The Ark was soon returned to the Israelites along with great treasures and gifts of gold. The calamities, which were on the Philistines while they possessed the Ark, went away as soon as they returned the Ark to Israel."

"So," said the Prime Minster, "you are telling us the power and greatness of Biblical Israel and our future is centered on the Ark of the Covenant?"

"Yes," replied Markus. "You see, the Ark is the place where God gave his instruction to Israel. To come before the Ark was to come before God's abiding presence. It led the chosen people to their next place of rest and scattered their enemies before them. Now that the Ark of the Covenant is no long in Israel's camp...to quote from 1 Samuel 4: 22: 'The Glory has departed from Israel, for the Ark of God has been captured.' When the Ark is with Israel, God is with Israel.

"I find the way the Philistines returned the Ark of God to Israel to be very interesting. Would you like to hear the story?" asked Dr. Markus.

"Yes, I would like to know as much as you are willing to share with us," said Zack.

Dr. Markus started, "Once it was decided to return the Ark, they knew it had to be done properly to remove the curse. They got a new cart and placed the Ark on it along with offerings of gold. Then two oxen that had recently given birth to calves were harnessed up to the cart. The calves were taken away and placed in a stall. Then the cart and oxen were placed on the road. The oxen started down the road mooing all the time, calling for their calves as they moved down the road away from their calves, pulling the cart back to the Israelites. It would be an accomplishment totally against the nature of the oxen to leave their calves, and another accomplishment if they found the way to the Israelites camp without help. The oxen pulled the cart directly to the Israelites' camp without making one wrong step. Interesting story isn't it?" said Dr. Markus. "Now let me get back to telling you about my research.

"To boil my theory down to the simplest terms I would tell you this. The Ark was given to "Israel". When Israel has possession of the Ark, God protects them. Israel will suffer when it does not have the Ark and even worse sufferings come to all others that take possession of the Ark."

"If we were to believe your theory, then what should we do about it?" asked the Defense Minister.

"You go get the Ark and bring it back to its rightful place," said the Professor.

"And just how do we do that? We don't know where the Ark is located; it has not been seen since the Temple in Jerusalem was destroyed some twenty-five hundred years ago. The things you have told us so far are things we have been taught since our childhood. What are we supposed to do with this information when we don't know where to find the Ark?"

"Just bear with me a few minutes," said Markus, "and you will see where this is going. The following information is where my research really comes together to reveal what must happen if Israel is to ever have the curse of not having the Ark removed.

"The story begins about three thousand years ago, when the Queen of Sheba is said to have ruled the land of Sheba, part of which is now Ethiopia. In those times, Sheba / Ethiopia was a vast and wealthy country extending across the Red Sea with seaports and trade throughout the known world. According to the Old Testament and a number of other documents, the Queen of Sheba, having heard of the wisdom and great wealth of King Solomon, went to Jerusalem to visit him. King Solomon welcomed the Queen of Sheba and she found favor in his court. The Bible tells of the great amount of treasure of gold and valuable spices she brought to King Solomon. It is believed she wanted to establish trade with Israel and make treaties with this powerful King.

"The Ethiopian chronicle Kebra Nagast written by Yetshak, an Ethiopian Monk, also relates the story of Makeda, the legendary Queen of Sheba. Makeda traveled to visit the wise King Solomon. She was very impressed with King Solomon and everything she saw and heard. She was so impressed that she accepted the religion and traditions of the Jews. King Solomon was attracted to the Queen's beauty and wisdom. He was overcome with desire for her and devised a plan to seduce her. King Solomon told the Queen she was welcome to anything in his Kingdom, but she must not take anything without asking first and receiving his permission. He then planned a banquet where a lot of spicy foods were served to the guests. In the night Makeda became very thirsty because of the spicy foods she had eaten and took a drink of water. King Solomon charged her with breaking his rule and violating his trust. He demanded and received sexual favors from her as payment.

"It is said that when Makeda returned home, she was pregnant with King Solomon's son, a child she named Menelik.

"When the boy grew up, he went to Jerusalem to see his father. King Solomon welcomed his son into his court where he studied the laws and faith of the Hebrews. Menelik stayed in Jerusalem approximately three years and then decided to return home. Solomon had the priest anoint him as the first Emperor of Ethiopia before he departed.

"Solomon was so taken with his son that he commanded the elders of Israel to send their firstborn sons with Menelik, and they took with them the Ark of the Covenant. Thus according to the story, the divine presence moved from Zion to Ethiopia. The city of Aksum still holds the tomb of the first Emperor of Ethiopia, Menelik; and hidden somewhere within the ancient Church of St Mary of Zion, the Ark of the Covenant is said to rest to this very day.

"The Koran, The Holy Book of Islam, and the Jewish Targum Sheni, a translation of the book of Esther, both relate similar stories of King Solomon and The Queen of Sheba," said Dr. Markus. "I have recently uncovered several other references to the meeting of these two rulers and all follow the same story line with only slight variations. Usually when we find the same story repeated from this many different sources it leads us to accept that the legend is based in truth. "

"To make my theory even stronger, let's look at what has happened in both Israel and Ethiopia after Menelik left Jerusalem with the Ark. First, soon after Menelik and the Ark of the Covenant left King Solomon, Israel started to decline with the attack of Jerusalem by the Egyptian king Shishak. The Temple was pillaged and the vast amount of treasures was taken away. The last vestige of King Solomon's kingdom vanished when King Nebuchadnezzar of Babylon completed the destruction of the temple. The Ark of the Covenant was not mentioned in either of these events. We would expect a treasure as important as the Ark to have been mentioned in some of these records if it had been destroyed or pillaged. Anyway, let us continue to look at what has happened to Israel since the Ark was taken away.

"To this very day, you can see one calamity after another that has been placed upon the Hebrew people. From Nazi Germany to the PLO, Israel has not known peace. Looking in the Old Testament again we read in 1 Samuel.4: 22: 'The Glory has departed from Israel.' I tell you, Israel will not see peace until the Glory or Ark of God is returned to its rightful place.'"

"Dr. Markus are you saying the holocaust was the result of Israel's not having the Ark of the Covenant?" asked the Prime Minster.

"I'm telling you that while Israel has possession of the Ark of the Covenant, God promised guidance and aid. The Ark of the Covenant led the Jewish nation in the wilderness and scattered their enemies before them. I believe God will protect Israel against all enemies when Israel follows God's will, and God's will was for Israel to have the Ark of the Covenant.

"Now let us consider what has happened to Ethiopia. It was a great and wealth country until the Ark of the Covenant came to their land. They soon were defeated in war and lost much of their lands and access to their seaports; being cut off from the sea, it lost the valuable trade routes. Ethiopia was over run by the Romans, suffered greatly during the Crusades, and much of the nation was forced to convert to Islam. Even today it is no longer the place of rich agriculture; instead it's a place of hunger, drought, war and famine. The Ethiopian people are very poor and suffer greatly, as did the Philistines when they possessed the Ark of God. As I said before, the Ark was given to Israel and every time another nation has taken control of it, both Israel and that nation have suffered.

"Then you believe the Ark of the Covenant is the reason for the suffering of both nations?" asked the Prime Minister.

"Yes! That's what I just said. As long as the Ark remains in Ethiopia the curse will cause much suffering to the Ethiopian people, and as long as Israel is without the Ark of God, it will continue to suffer. You must go retrieve the Ark of the Covenant if you want your enemies to be scattered before you and peace to return to the Hebrews. But I must warn you, if you decide to retrieve the Ark, it must be done in the correct way or even greater suffering will come upon Israel.

"I would be happy to tell you what must be done to assure your safety when and if you make the decision to return the Glory to Israel. You decide, then call me if you want my help. Now if you would be so kind to have those – uh, 'gentlemen-- return me to my work."

After Dr. Markus left, the office of the Minister of Defense became very busy. Several members of the group thought the Doctor was an idiot, some thought him to be just plain crazy, but the Prime Minister was not so sure and gave a lot of thought before he made his response. Finally he spoke and said, "When you think about it and consider all that has happened to our people it all seems possible. I don't see that we would have anything to lose by looking into this theory. Have someone contact a Rabbi, run this by him, and get one of our best Professors at the university to check out the good Doctor's theory. We'll meet again tomorrow and consider this further."

Chapter 6

The more Prime Minster Benjamin thought about it the more he became convinced that if the Ark did exist and it was in Ethiopia as Dr. Markus had related, then the theory could have some validity. He would see what his people would discover and make a decision tomorrow. One thing was for certain, something had to be done to stop the killing and protect his people. This something had to be more than just blowing some old buildings and keeping the General in his house for a few days.

The morning started with the usual reports being read over his morning coffee, but his mind was not on the reports. The Prime Minster was still thinking about what Dr. Markus has told him. It all was becoming clearer the more he thought about it, but he would wait and see what his experts uncovered in their research.

It was about noon before members of the Security Council gathered to receive the reports from the experts. Some of the experts said the Ark had been destroyed with the Temple in 586 BC, but there was no record to prove this statement to be true. One report said the Ark of the Covenant was buried in the hills around Jerusalem. Another thought it had been pillaged and destroyed when the Temple was ransacked. But all of the reports had one thing in common: There is a lot of evidence that the Queen of Sheba did visit King Solomon and that she did return home pregnant. It is also true that Menelik was the first Emperor of Ethiopia and his tomb is at Aksum.

Legend is strong in support of the Ark of the Covenant being sent with Menelik back to Sheba, which at that time was part of Ethiopia we know today. The people of Ethiopia openly claim that the Ark is in the Church of St Mary and there are many ancient Ethiopian manuscripts that support this claim. Just last summer excavations of a wall at Abba-Pantleon in Aksum uncovered inscriptions that revealed the instructions for the safe keeping of the Ark of God. There is much more to this report, but it appears the good Dr. Markus may be on to something.

"OK!" said the Prime Minster. "Will the Ethiopian Government give us the Ark if they have it?"

"No," said the experts, "it is said to be their most valued treasure."

"Has anyone seen the Ark; do they have any pictures to support their claim?"

"No," replied the expert. "The Ark is guarded day and night by a single monk, named Abba Mekonen.

Known as the Atang, the keeper of the Ark, he is 69 years old, very frail and bone thin. It is a great honor and a terrible burden to be chosen to this most solemn post. He is chosen for life, takes an oath to guard and protect the Ark of the Covenant, and will never leave the chapel compound. When asked why no one could see the Ark, he replies simply, 'Who can look on the face of God.' If the Ark is not there, then this is the biggest hoax ever played on a whole nation and it has lasted for over three thousand years," said the expert.

"Thank you for your report," Prime Minster Benjamin told all the people gathered in his office. "Please understand that you are not to reveal anything concerning this meeting. I will contact you when and if we want any further research done."

As soon as the room was empty, Benjamin picked up the phone and told his secretary to contact Dr. Markus and have him come to a meeting of the Security Council at 9:30 the following morning. Dr. Markus had already cleared his calendar, for he was expecting the call.

The meeting started at 9:30 AM sharp with all members of the Security Council present along with Dr. Markus. The Prime Minster spoke first saying to Dr. Markus, "I will admit you have given us much to ponder since our meeting yesterday. It appears the things you told us are correct as best that we can confirm. Now that we accept your theory as possible, what or how do we use this information to make our country more secure?"

Dr. Markus smiled and nodded to the Prime Minster, "You proceed very carefully to return the Ark to its rightful place, but first let me warn you. It is very important that no human blood is shed in your effort to get the Ark. By reading the Old Testament concerning the Ark you will find details that should be followed when approaching the Ark. Let me remind you of some of the rules that are to be followed. The people of Aksum have been very loyal in attending to the Ark and keeping it safe and they must not be harmed in any way. In fact they should be given gifts of great value as reward for protecting the Ark over the centuries. The only people that can attend the Ark in transportation are Priests, and they should be from the ancient tribe of Levy. They must purify themselves before approaching the Ark of God as described in Exodus. No one must touch the Ark at any time, for to do so will cause death. The Ark is to be covered with animal skin and then a blue cloth. It is to be carried on the shoulders, using the poles that are in the rings of each side, and by all means no one is to open or look inside of the chest. As you may remember, when the Philistines returned the Ark of the Covenant to Israel, seventy men looked inside the chest and they all died a horrible death."

"OK, how do we find out whom among us are descendants of the tribe of Levy?" asked Zack.

"That part of this operation will be fairly easy," said Dr. Markus. "We have found the burial site of a Priest with inscriptions bearing the mark of the tribe of Levy. The mummy's remains have readable DNA, and this can be used to match the DNA of those chosen for this mission."

"Just what is supposed to be inside the Ark?" asked one of the council members.

Dr. Markus replied, "The two stone tables that Moses brought down from Mt. Sinai with the Ten Commandments written on them, a jar containing manna which God fed the people of Israel while they wandered in the wilderness, possibly the rod of Aaron, and maybe the old book of law. Although some of these items may have been removed or never actually placed inside the chest, we do know the stone tablets and the jar of manna were placed inside."

Someone asked, "Do we know exactly what this Ark looks like?"

We have a relief of a chest on a cart that was uncovered a few years ago in the ruins of Capernaum. This chest matches the size and type given for the Ark of the Covenant. We are not sure this is an exact likeness, but it will give you an idea of what it will look like. "I have a picture of this relief in my briefcase, which I will give you," said Dr. Markus as he dug into his leather case.

After a few minutes of deep thought, the Prime Minster cleared his throat and said. "Dr. Markus, we have decided to see if the Ark of The Covenant is in Aksum as you have told us, and if it is we are going to attempt to bring it home to its rightful place. Now how would you recommend we proceed with this venture?"

Dr. Markus smiled and said, "Very carefully".

Chapter 7

Captain Brady is head of Israel Army's Special Forces. He is a strong man and excellent leader. The last twelve years of military service have proven his dedication to his country. He has led many successful secret-missions and has distinguished himself in combat. He is also engaged to marry the Prime Minster's youngest daughter, Rachel, in the fall. His future looks very good; with his loyal service to his country and the political connections of his future father-in-law; he could hold a high government office when he retires. The captain has been chosen to take on another very secret mission.

Rachel had asked her father not to allow Captain Brady to take on any more dangerous missions. Her love for the captain has continued to grow from the first day they met. Rachel is a gentle soul and a very caring person. Captain Brady and she are different in almost every way. He is tall, strong, adventurous, and can be a very dangerous person when the need for such conduct is needed. His fierce and savage actions in combat have earned him many medals and rewards for valor from his men and country. Rachel, on the other hand, is soft, gentle, caring, and would not harm an insect. She spends most of her time helping the poor and sick. Though they are very different their deep love for each other is known to all that know them. They have been planning their marriage and future life together for several months. They have already found a lovely cottage where they will live and raise their children, hopefully a boy and a girl.

Rachel has promised to marry the captain, but not until he retires from the military. She could not live a good life thinking of the bad things that could happen to her husband if he were still in the Army. She did not want to be a young widow like many of her friends.

When Captain Brady told Rachel of the upcoming mission, he told her it would be a very safe routine mission and would not involve combat. He gave her his word and promised to be careful and return to her safely. Her father had needed someone he could trust to do this mission and had asked Captain Brady. Would her father have asked if it were dangerous? This will be Captain Brady's last mission, then retirement from the Army and marriage to his lovely Rachel.

Captain Brady is working on direct orders of the Prime Minister to assemble an elite special unit for a very secret mission. The order he received for this mission contained some very unusual directives. Several members of the unit must be able to trace their heritage back to the tribe of Levy and have it confirmed with a DNA test. The unit is to consist of at least two priests. There are to be twelve men on the team as specialists in communications, transportation, weapons, martial arts, and explosives. Provisions were to be made for handling some very delicate but deadly merchandise. Arranging for these special provisions in total secret was no small order in itself, but he was given only twenty days to select, train and prepare this special unit, and for what? He was not told.

The twelve men assembled were the very best of the best. Each had been chosen for his special talent and his bloodline. Brady is a leader with a reputation of getting the job done and this fact was known by all in attendance. He had been given the job of getting this group of people to work, act, and perform as a unit. For Captain Brady this was business as usual, but what really baffled him was the special order that all the training was to be done with non-lethal weapons. He thought it was child's play to train such a special group of warriors using only stun guns, rubber bullets, and hand to hand combat. The directive to train in secret with special gas masks and night vision scopes added even more puzzlement to his unasked questions. Captain Brady was a loyal soldier and understood his job was not to reason why, his job was to obey orders and get the Unit ready for what ever was coming.

Mark would be second in command of the unit and like Captain Brady had been recognized for his bravery in several conflicts. He was known as a fierce warrior and would be first to the enemy attack and the last to leave any fight. His loyalty to the mission, his country, and faith in his God was the guide of his life.

Tim was in charge of the communications and had been a close friend of Captain Brady. He often joked with Captain Brady about Rachel and would tell him, "If you won't marry Rachel, I will." Brady was not sure this was a joke. He knew most men and that all of his friends would jump at a chance to wed his beloved Rachel

Captain Brady did not personally know the other members of the Unit, but he had reviewed their records and knew everyone of them could handle whatever was coming.

The two priests were the only weak links and Brady had voiced his concerns about priests being part of a military mission. He had been told that they were a major part of the mission and to train them for the mission and not question the part they would play. Their role would be apparent when the time came for them to act. The priests spent a lot of time reading some old documents and making notes. They kept to themselves when not training and were often talking to each other in hushed tones and making strange looking items from animal skins and purple cloth. Once they were observed mixing some strange substance to make a sweet smelling perfume. Questions about what they were doing and why these things were needed, would go unanswered. Even though the captain had been told not to question the actions of the priests, it was very hard to obey when they butchered and burned a male sheep. The ram was drained of its blood, skinned, washed in water, and cut into parts. The different parts were burned and the blood was put into a vessel and sprinkled around a stone table while the priests chanted a strange song-like verse in an ancient form of the Hebrew language. The members of the Unit were told this was all part of the priests' training for the upcoming mission.

The training went well with each member of the group accepting his position on the team. They worked hard to hone their skills and prepare for the coming mission. Sometimes there were questions between members of the group about the coming mission and some speculation about what was going to happen, but there were never any real answers.

Nearing the end of the training, Captain Brady was called into office of the Minister of Defense, and to his surprise was greeted by his future father-in-law, Prime Minster Benjamin. He asked if the Unit was trained and ready. Captain Brady told him they were ready for most anything and were working together as one. Prime Minster Benjamin asked if the captain had spoken with his daughter and he told him that he had not talked with her since the training began. His orders had been to train for a secret mission and no member of the Unit was allowed to contact anyone out side the Unit. The Prime Minster dropped his head and said, "I will let my daughter know you are well and will call her soon."

The Prime Minster told Brady of the coming mission and expressed upon him the special circumstances of it. The captain had a few expected questions concerning the mission, but never once questioned the mission itself. If his Prime Minster thought this was a mission that would benefit his country, he would see to it that his orders were carried out or die trying.

There were others interested in the training of the Unit. It's always hard to keep a secret in this part of the world. The word had gone out very quickly that something was going to happen, that a special Unit had been formed and some very unusual training was taking place. Orders were issued to find out what this was all about.

Chapter 8

When the day to start the mission finally came, the Unit was gathered in an aircraft hanger and briefed on their objectives. The Unit was issued old clothing, mostly rags, which were robe-like garments with pockets sown on the inside where their weapons and other equipment could be concealed. The large equipment was placed in an old crate, which was put on an old wooden handcart that already had several cages containing small animals on it. Then everything was loaded on the waiting Black Hawk.

Once the aircraft was en route each man was given a bottle of body lotion with a dark stain in it. They were to apply this lotion over their entire body to darken their skin color. It quickly became apparent they would have the appearance of a group of black men. Matt, the medic for the Unit said, "My black American friend told me if I was ever black for one Saturday night that I would never be white again."

Sam laughed as he applied the lotion, saying, "Yeah, and I'm going to apply it extra heavy to my Johnson to see what will happen." They all laughed at the jokes to help relieve the tension that comes before every mission.

In short order they settled down. Now dressed in their old ragged robes they could easily pass for black men, at least they could from a distance.

The uneventful flight took place after midnight and ended when the Black Hawk landed on a flat stretch of deserted land alongside Ethiopia's Lake Tana. The aircraft was quickly unloaded and left the area within a few minutes. The group of men that remained on the ground gave the appearance of being Ethiopian Christians who were making a pilgrimage to worship at any one of the country's shrines. The Unit would meet several similar small bands of worshipers on the road over the next few days. Dressed as they were the Unit blended in and could easily pass for any one of these groups.

They quickly set up a crude campsite with a tent made from old worn animal skins and settled in for the night. Guards were set up to protect the Unit against uninvited guests.

The morning started early when a small campfire was built and coffee, breakfast, and plans for the day were made.

This first morning they had to find a boat to take them on the two hours boat ride across Lake Tana to the isolated monastery called Tana Kirkos. There are approximately thirty Christian monks at the monastery, which stands at the tip of a long peninsula. This is where legend says Menelik first brought the Ark of the Covenant to Ethiopia. The plan called for the Unit to follow the same route that the Ark of the Covenant took, all the way to Aksum. This route is often traveled by worshipers, so the Unit would not attract attention as it made its way to recover the Ark of the Covenant.

Captain Brady knew from maps of the area that a small fishing village was located a short distance from the landing zone. He had most of his men remain at the campsite and continue posing as local worshipers on a pilgrimage. The guards were relieved and told to get some rest while other members of the Unit would be alert should uninvited guests happen upon them.

Captain Brady took two men with him and hiked to the fishing village to hire a boat to take them across Lake. It was nearing midmorning when the fishermen began pushing their boats into the water and preparing for the day's work. Brady approached one of the fishermen as he was getting into his boat, which was larger that any of the others. After a few minutes the deal was struck and they were in the boat moving down the lake.

It took about an hour to arrive at the campsite of the Unit and to load the men and gear on the boat. They understood from the fisherman that he had made this trip many times before, carrying worshipers across the Lake. The money for this taxi service was more than he would make all week fishing, so he would be happy to help them. The craft was almost overloaded and sat low in the water as they began the trip across the lake.

The boat was very old and in bad need of painting. The motor sputtered and smoked but pushed the boat across the smooth surface of the lake with ease. The ride over to Tana Kirkos started uneventfully as some of the men slept while others kept watch. They did not expect trouble, but Brady had learned the hard way always to expect the unexpected, and there were bands of local bandits ready to take advantage of the careless. It would not be good if some local thief tried to hold up this skilled group of warriors and got his ass kicked.

It was near noon when the motor of the boat started to smoke and cough heavily. It soon stopped running and glided to a stop. The shoreline could be seen in the distance but it would be impossible to manually paddle this large a boat to shore. Captain Brady had a feeling this was just the beginning of his bad luck.

A cloud of black foul smelling smoke bellowed out as the fisherman opened the hatch to begin working on the engine. It did not look promising to Captain Brady, but the fisherman did not appear alarmed as he gathered his tools and started to clunk around on the engine.

"Look there!" said one of the men on watch. "Is that a patrol boat heading this way?"

Captain Brady strained to make out the object in the distance that was moving in their general direction. After a few seconds he said, "Yes, it is one of the Ethiopian Government's modern patrol boats and it's definitely coming in our direction. He quietly told his men, "Remain calm and let the fisherman do the talking. I'm sure we haven't been discovered .The patrol boat is only coming to give aid to the disabled boat."

The patrol boat pilot pulled along side of the fishing boat and cut his engine. There were four young soldiers standing on the deck of the patrol boat and they were giving the people on the fishing boat close scrutiny. Captain Brady did not see any weapons and saw nothing in the soldiers' actions to give him alarm.

The fisherman stepped forward and spoke with the soldiers briefly. He told them the fuel line had broken and had sprayed diesel fuel on the engine. This had caused the engine to stop and smoke to bellow out of the engine compartment. They had been lucky it had not caught on fire or exploded. He asked the soldiers if they could give him a tow to the nearest shore so he could clean up the spilled fuel and make repairs.

The soldier said they could and threw a line to the stricken fishing vessel and was soon towing it toward the shore.

As the boat approached the rocky shore, Captain Brady could easily see the Monastery. It is hard to believe this structure was several centuries old and had always been inhabited. He could not see any of the people he knew would be at the Monastery.

When the boats got within a hundred feet of shore, the patrol boat picked up speed, then withdrew the towrope and turned, moving back out to the center of the Lake. The soldiers waved to the fisherman and the Unit as the momentum carried the fishing vessel to shore.

The Unit quickly unloaded the fishing boat and helped the fisherman splice the fuel line. They waited on the shore as the fisherman restarted his engine and began the return trip across the Lake.

As the fisherman departed, the group of men climbed the peninsula's cliffs. They were met by some of the Monks that lived at the monastery. The Monks were wearing purple and red turban-like hats, long colorful robes, and many were holding umbrellas that symbolized the heavens. Captain Brady became alarmed when he saw the long wooden poles some of the monks were carrying. He thought the poles were used as weapons, but soon found out these were prayer sticks used to lean on when the monks would pray for hours. These monks met everyone traveling near the monastery hoping to receive a donation and offered a blessing in return. The Unit had made provisions for this type of contact and gave the monks a small bag of salt and a bag of dried beans. The blessing given the Unit was brief and chanted clearly by the old monk. He chanted, "May God give you aid in your endeavor and safety in your travel." Captain Brady thought how appropriate this blessing was to his mission.

The monastery building was something out of the Middle Ages, carved from the soft volcanic rock of the area. Brady was later to find out there were twelve of these churches, all built over a thousand years ago, and eleven of them had been discovered and inhabited from that time. Only one of these buildings still remained undiscovered, if there ever were twelve churches as the legend told. Several monks stood along the outer walls of the monastery chanting prayers and paid very little attention to the Unit.

The Unit kept to themselves as they passed the monastery and went through the small village without incident. Only a small dog came out of the village, barked a few times, and then trotted back to lie in the shade of a small bush. The locals were accustomed to seeing strangers and small groups of people moving about the countryside.

The Unit made an overnight camp a short distance from the small village. They would eat and get a few hours rest tonight. They could easily have traveled all night, but to do this could attract attention. It was better to travel and rest as any other travelers would.

Captain Brady thought of his beloved Rachel as he lay on his bedroll waiting for sleep to overtake him. He thought about how much he loved her and how they were as different as day is from night. She is a very lovely person with a soft soul, always looking out for others. She works with those injured and the families of those killed by the bombings. She has always had a place in her heart for anyone in pain. Sometime Captain Brady could not understand how someone like Rachel could love a person like him. He was a hard man, a warrior. He had killed and had caused pain and suffering in others. How lucky could a person like him be by being favored with the love of this woman?

Chapter 9

Morning came quickly with the sun jumping from the horizon. During the day the temperature became very warm, as they were only fourteen degrees from the equator and nearly nine thousand feet high. The plan was for them to travel from Tana Kirkos to Lalibela nearly one hundred miles away. They started out along a rarely traveled back road that had been used by pilgrims for many centuries. The road turned out to be only a dirt trail, used mostly by foot traffic and carts pulled by hand or oxen. The few motor vehicles in this area were mostly old military trucks and were frequently seen broken down along the roadside. Captain Brady was glad he had the GPS unit to keep him from getting lost. He could see how easy it would be to become turned around in this desolate country. Except for a few minor variations the terrain every place looked alike. Most of the area was brown and looked as if it had not ever seen rainfall. Everything just looked dry, dusty, and dead.

They traveled by a small patchwork farm where a farmer was using a plow, which was made of sticks.

The plow was being pulled by thin sickly oxen as they have done for hundreds of years. The main crop appeared to be teff, a small drought resistant grain that is the staple of the Ethiopian diet. The grain is made into sour bread called injera, which is traditionally baked on a large clay pan over a cow dung fire. The men of the Unit preferred their cold MRE's (meals ready to eat) to anything cooked on a cow dung fire.

The few houses they had seen were made of stones and mud that had been stacked together. Building materials are scarce for there are very few trees and these are really only a few small brown bushes. The countryside is a very desolate wilderness and heavily rock-strewn. The evidence of poverty and the desperation of the people is seen everywhere. It's as if the land itself has been cursed for a very long time.

The Unit had to be ever watchful for land mines and was forced to move only on the heavily used and rutted roads or paths. This part of Ethiopia has been in a civil war that has ravaged the country for a hundred years, and even now sometimes they could hear the faint sound of gunfire off in the distance. Traveling in this terrain is done only at a very slow pace. It will take them several days to reach Aksum and the Ark of the Covenant.

The first full day's trek from Lake Tana had been long and hot; the men were ready for the coolness the night would bring. It is always hard to understand how the temperature in the desert can be so hot during the day and then turn so awfully cold during the night. The men sat around the small fire eating the MRE's, drank strong coffee, and marveled at the beautiful night sky. It is a considerable contrast between the beauty and the harshness of this country. It is easy to see what a great place this could be if it just had regular rain fall and a government that is not corrupt.

Tomorrow they would reach Lalibela, a modern town with several holy sites where worshipers come to pray. The Unit will slow down as it approaches these sites and take on the posture of other travelers on the road. It is very important that they not attract attention to themselves. They hoped to have the advantage of surprise when the time came to locate the Ark, acquire the Ark, and get out of the country without a fight.

It looked as if this whole country was a place time had forgotten. They had seen very little of the modern world since they left the Lake, if you could call the old boat and motor modern. Even the military trucks and the soldiers' weapons they had seen on the road were of World War II era, and they were usually broken down.

The men of the Unit had plenty of time to think as they walked down the rough road. Captain Brady thought about his beautiful Rachel and made plans for when he would hold her in his arms again. He could imagine the home that he and Rachel would buy and the children that were sure to make his life perfect. He had loved Rachel for many years but had not told her until last year. They had attended the same school, but he had not known her then, for she was several years younger then he. They had met again last year when her father was sworn in to office. They had fallen in love almost at once and had been seeing each other whenever they could arrange to meet. They always had to be careful because of her father's position in the government. There was always someone that would try to use his relationship with Rachel to get at her father. Captain Brady had promised Rachel that he would get out of the Army before their marriage and get a regular job. This could and probably would be his last mission as an Army Officer.

The priest thought of the history of this country and could not understand what had happened to make these people so desperate. What had happened to make this country so cursed? They knew the ancient history of this area and the riches that once abounded within the borders. There had not been any signs of progress or hope so far on this venture. How could this country with so much history and past wealth become so desolate? They thought they knew the answer, but only time would tell.

Each man walked with his own thoughts as they made their way across country.

The road dropped down into a valley-like area that appeared to be an old lakebed. Captain Brady knew this was all that remained of the huge reservoir that once furnished water for this whole region. The water from the Blue Nile would flow into this reservoir and would be used in times of little or no rain. This valley was once lush and green with many crops and forests. Wild animals, birds, and fish abounded in the area and furnished food to the many inhabitants of the valley. The people of the valley were very industrious and would trade food and crafts with other people in the country and even to other parts of the known world. They became very wealthy and life was comfortable and carefree. Now it was as desolate as any they had traveled in this impoverished country.

Captain Brady knew they were getting close to Lalibela when the land began to turn from brown, dry, and dusty to light green and they finally came to the upper reaches of the Blue Nile River. This is the first area they crossed that even gave the appearance that it could support any form of comfortable life. They would not need a boat to cross the Blue Nile River. It is not a river as one would believe; instead it is only a wide shallow muddy ditch in this area. The River at one time had been a wide flowing stream that furnished the whole area with water for the farmers' crops and animals. Today and in recent history it is only a wide mud hole due to the lack of rain fall in the area. This whole country had experienced terrible draught and famine for thousands of centuries.

There were a few moments of concern when the cart became bogged down in the mud along the river. It took all the muscle the men of the Unit could muster to dislodge the cart and get it to firmer ground. They were now covered in mud on top of the dust and sweat that had covered them during the last two days. The Unit now looked exactly like the native people.

As the Unit drew near Lalibela each member of the Unit became aware of the unusual sounds and a strange sweet scent in the air. They soon passed a church that must have been many centuries old. The building was all below ground level and appeared to have been carved in one piece out of bedrock. The windows along the sides of the building were cut in the shape of the cross. Smoke from burning incense billowed from each of these windows making it look as if the building were on fire. This is where the sweet smell in the air came from. The unusual sound came from a small group of monks along the side of the church. They were leaning on wooden poles while chanting prayers read from worn prayer books. The walkways and steps around the church were deeply worn by the many centuries of traffic from bare feet worshipers.

Lalibela is much like Tana Kirkos with very old buildings, many of which were constructed by the Romans or were built during the Crusades. Lalibela is the site of several religious shrines, some of them twenty-five hundred years old. As the Unit made its way along the outskirts of the village, it drew attention form several of the local monks. They came with prayer sticks in hand, seeking donations of food or money, and offered a blessing in return. Rabbi Hiram met the monks and after several minutes of conversation gave them a few coins. These monks spoke a few words of blessing that were not understood by anyone in the Unit, then turned and walked away. Monks seeking food in return for a blessing is a common occurrence. The Unit could expect more of this type of encounter any time they were near a village or city.

As the monks went away, Captain Brady could feel the tension in his neck. This mission had been too easy, everything was working too smoothly, and he could feel trouble coming. He had experienced this feeling before, and paying attention to it had saved his life. He would remain very alert for the remainder of this mission.

With Lalibela growing small in the distance behind them, the Unit turned north and headed toward Aksum. They found traveling much easier when they kept closer to the Blue Nile River. The temperature seemed to cool a few degrees with the added moisture in the air from the river. Even a cooling shade could be found under the small bushes which dotted the way every now and then. When they stopped for the night many of the men took advantage of the warm waters of the Blue Nile to clean off some of the mud, sweat, and dust that they had caked on them. They would rest here eight hours tonight and get some hot food and rest from the two days of walking in the almost unbearable heat. Captain Brady looked over each of his men; he wanted them well rested when they got to Aksum. He was not the only one watching his men, but he did not know it.

Chapter 10

The following morning Captain Brady gathered all the men of the Unit together and went over the plan with each man to make sure everyone knew exactly what was expected. He told them that they were approximately thirty miles from Aksum and that they would travel this distance today, stopping just outside the ancient town. There they would rest until it became dark. The scouts would then be sent in to check things out and to locate the Chapel of St. Mary. Once the scouts returned with the location of the chapel and information on the town, a plan of attack would be drawn up. They broke camp and turned north away from the river and began to travel the last miles to Aksum.

The terrain quickly changed back to the hot, dry, and desolate desert, like they had traveled through earlier in the mission. Ever so often a small dry patch gave the appearance of once being cultivated for farming, but no crops were seen now. A thin sick looking cow could be seen eating the dry brown grass found beside the road and one bird was seen circling in the distance. One of the men was heard to say, "This is truly the most God-forsaken land in the world." Captain Brady would agree with this statement if anyone had asked him. He had seen the pictures on the television of the famine, drought, and civil war that ravaged this country. He would quickly change the channel when they showed the starving children with swollen bellies and flies at the edge of their eyes and mouths. Looking at this place, he could not understand how anybody could live here. He had seen a lot of bad things in his many years of military service and he knew the innocent always suffered in time of war, but this place was worse than anything else he could imagine. Here there was no hope for anything to get better; he wanted only to finish the mission and get out of this cursed country.

He wished he were back home with his beloved Rachel, planning for the happy times that were sure to come in the very near future. In his mind he could see her dressed in her wedding dress and the pink flowers that would accent her lovely hair. She would make herself more beautiful, if that were possible, just for him. Then would come their first night together, but he could not think of these things while in this God-forsaken place. If there was ever hell on earth, this place had to be it. It was as if the very land itself and everything in it had been cursed.

Mid morning found them hot, sweat-covered, and careless. They rounded a sharp curve in the road and found themselves confronted by three armed men. Captain Brady had seen one of these men near the last village but had not paid attention to him. They demanded money for safe passage and threatened the Unit if they did not comply. Captain Brady told his men to unload some of the cargo from the cart and at the same time positioned himself between the bandits. His men soon realized what he was doing. The bandits could not fire their weapons at the Unit unless they chanced hitting each other. The members of the Unit quickly took advantage of the situation and disarmed the bandits, with two of them rendered unconscious by the stun guns.

"Now what are we going to do with these idiots?" asked one of Captain Brady's men.

Captain Brady told them to move them off the road and tie them securely. He wanted to silence them for good, but he remembered his orders that "no human blood can be shed". These stupid people were causing a problem for the Unit and a solution had to be found quickly. He could not allow them to be released, for they would surely reveal that a group of soldiers was posing as pilgrims. Nor could he go against orders and kill them as he would have liked.

He decided to make the bandits come with them until they reached the halfway point to Aksum.

Then, he mused, "I'll untie them and send them back unarmed and without food or water. It would take these idiots about two days to make the trip back and they probably would not talk about getting their butts kicked anyway. What would they say? "We were robbing some pilgrims and they took our guns and kicked our asses". Who would they tell, the Police? I don't think so!"

As they neared Aksum they saw it was a smaller village than some of the other towns they had passed along the way. One could not help being impressed by the nearly seventy feet tall geometrically carved obelisk that marked the royal tombs of Aksum. Some of these obelisks were over two thousand years old, and the only sign of age or exposure to the elements is seen in a slight tilt to one side. One of these obelisks marks the burial site of King Solomon's and The Queen of Sheba's son, Menelik, who brought the Ark of the Covenant to Ethiopia and was the first Emperor of Sheba. Rumors are that the bloodline of King Solomon has ruled Ethiopia uninterrupted until about thirty years ago.

Arriving late in the day, the Unit quickly made camp and waited for darkness to set upon them. The scouts made their way into the village as the people began to settle in for the night. They found the village much like all the others, with narrow streets, rundown shacks, and the signs of poverty everywhere. There were many crosses and the Star of David displayed all over the village, making it quite evident that these are a very religious people. The display of the many crosses was the result of the Christian Crusades, and the Star of David from the Jewish influence.

The Chapel of St. Mary was easily located since it is a well kept modern building sitting in the middle of the village. A strong iron fence about nine feet tall protects the chapel and its surrounding courtyard. There were no guards or police officers seen in this part of the village. After a few hours of watching the habits of the town's people and locating several escape routes, the scouts made their way back to the Unit and made the report to Captain Brady.

Upon listening to the report, Captain Brady decided that entering the chapel was going to be a piece of cake. It was time to make the final preparations for getting into the chapel and getting out of town without causing a disturbance. Captain Brady knew a disturbance would bring every man, woman, and child running to protect the treasures of the church.

The two priests and four men assigned to attend and carry the Ark were told to prepare themselves. The other members of the Unit began to unpack the special equipment from the crates stored on the old cart.

The priest and four chosen men withdrew from the other members of the Unit and began the cleansing process that is stated in detail in the Bible book of Leviticus. The priest began with the ritual washing, and then they were all anointed with holy oil. This oil was made using pure myrrh, sweet cinnamon, sweet calamus, cassia, and a hin of olive oil, following the instruction found in Exodus 30:23. The cleansing process would take two hours or more. Along with the many prayers, the ritual washing, the anointing of the Holy Oil, came the burnt offering of the young ram that had been brought along for this purpose. This ram had to have come from the flocks of Israel and had to be the first born and without blemish. The ram's blood was collected in a vessel of pure gold and would be used once the Ark of God was discovered.

The priest dressed in white linen undergarments under their old robes. They then put the priestly robes and breastplates that are made of gold in special backpacks made for this purpose. Instructions for these priestly garments are found in many of the old books and manuscripts. Along with these instructions came the warnings for anyone not following each and every detail of the instructions.

According to old manuscripts, it is very important that anyone just looking upon the Ark of the Covenant be clean and in good favor with God or he would die. In time of old, whenever a priest would approach the Ark, a rope would be tied to his right foot and bells were tied to the hem of his robe. If the bells stopped ringing or the priest was not found to be in good favor with God and was struck dead, the others could drag him back. The priests of the Unit had knowledge of these stories and were very careful to follow each step of the ritual.

While the Priests proceeded with their work, the other members of the Unit were busy. The gear was quickly unloaded and the night vision gear, knock out gas, gas masks, and weapons loaded with non-lethal ammo were passed out to each member of the Unit. Each man was given a headset communication radio. Two of the men were given small hand held medal detectors. After all the gear was given out, the men stored the equipment under their robes and settled down to get a few hours rest before the coming mission. There would be very little time for rest during the next twelve hours as the Unit made its escape, hopefully with the Ark.

A single dog barked somewhere in the village and every member of the Unit settled down with his thoughts.

Chapter 11

The mission began sometime after midnight with the members of the Unit moving out by groups of two or three, taking up assigned positions at key areas around the small village. When everyone was in position Captain Brady, the two priests, and the men with the metal detectors moved in position near the fence at the rear of the chapel. They removed the old robes that covered their black uniforms. They wanted the old monk to report to the authorities, that the Ark of God was taken by black men in military uniforms. This way the police and Ethiopian Government would be looking for a military unit that broke into the chapel not a small band of local travelers.

They soon began to work on the fence. It took only a few minutes to remove a small section of the fence and for the group of men to take up positions inside the courtyard of the chapel. Once inside Captain Brady announced over the radio that they were inside the compound, and then directed the men to a door in the rear of the building. This is where the Atang, the old Monk lived. It's very important to subdue him without injury or causing any noise that would alert the village, Captain Brady reminded. Surprisingly the door was found to be unlocked and entry into the living quarters of the chapel was made without problem.

The Atang was in his small room sleeping on a mat placed upon the floor, a small table was in the corner with a unlit candle, a well used prayer book, and a glass of water on it. The walls were bare with only a crude cross hanging by a leather strap is on one wall. The odor of incense was strong, but none was burning in this room. The monk looked very old and frail as he slept peacefully on his humble bed. Captain Brady began to feel bad at what he was going to do next.

The old man awoke and stared at the strange men that were crowded in his small sleeping quarters. His lack of alarm was disquieting as Captain Brady stepped forward to assure him that he would not be harmed. As the other members of the Unit spread though out the chapel it became evident the old monk was the only one in the building. The chapel was a stone building approx. one hundred feet by seventy-five feet with one large room in the front and several smaller rooms located closer to the back. The larger room with it high ceiling was decorated with crude paintings of people dressed in colorful robes attending to other people dressed in white with a glowing heads. The men understood these to be Ethiopian Saints or other important religious people. There are several crosses, statues, and candle holders along the walls. Located in the front of the larger room was a table or altar on which sat a candle stand and a golden cup. There were several heavily smoke- stained incense burners in the chapel and one was still smoking. Behind the table a large cross stands in front of a purple curtain which hung from the ceiling to the floor.

The priest could not help but notice the presents of the crosses in this chapel. It appears these people have combined the Christian and Jewish faiths. He had heard of the Black Jews of Ethiopia but had not really given much thought as to whom they are or just what they believed. This was truly a strange mix of the Old Testament and New Testament religions. The lay out of the chapel resembled that of a Temple and the cross was the influence of Christianity and the crusades.

Moving in front of the altar, Captain Brady said, "Could it be this easy? Could the Ark of God just be setting behind this purple curtain? They had expected that the Ark would be concealed in a wall or floor and thus it would be necessary to use the medal detectors to locate it. The men with the detectors had already begun searching the floors and walls with the small devices. There was a faint beep when the detectors moved over a nail or other metal object.

The Atang spoke for the first time as Captain Brady approached the curtain. Who among you may look upon the face of God? Everyone stopped in his tracks. Something about the calmness of his voice and the way he spoke these words caused a chill to come on everyone in the room.

Captain Brady spoke breaking the uneasy silence, telling the priests to proceed with the necessary steps to approach the Ark of the Covenant. The priests began by unpacking the robes with the bells and breastplates of gold. They quickly dressed and then began the ancient ritual of sprinkling blood from the sacrificed sheep upon the altar and repeating the prayers of old. It was strange hearing them use the Hebrew words of ancient Israel that they had first seen written on the Dead Sea Scrolls. The old monk watched the priest closely as they went about this ritual of preparation. He seemed to smile slightly as the blood is sprinkled on the altar and the nervous priest looked at each other as they very tentatively they moved behind the curtain. Both priests quickly backed from behind the curtain with the look of astonishment and fear on their faces. "It's not there," said one of the priests after a few seconds.

Captain Brady though disappointed, had not expected the Ark to just be waiting on displace for him. He ordered his men to continue searching for walls and floors for any evidence of a hidden passage.

The search went on for nearly an hour with no good results, only a few possible hiding places were found and they were quickly search and found to be empty or contained only ancient records of Ethiopian Saints. With the exception of a few small golden ornaments and some old manuscripts there was very little of value inside the building.

The Unit was ready to give up the search and accept that the story Ark of the Covenant being in Ethiopia was only a legend. He thought that it had either never been in Ethiopia or it had been moved many years ago. Captain Brady noticed the old monk kept looking at the floor just below the altar. As Captain Brady began looking closely at the pattern of the brick on the floor in this area he saw a brick which sat a little out of line of the others. He pulled his survival knife and inserted it the space around the brick and it came loose and moved to one side. Under this loose brick was a steel rod with a cable attached. As Captain Brady pulled the rod as loud click was heard and the altar and the floor below it began to slide backward. The floor opened about four feet and stopped. The opening below the altar was the beginning of a stairway cut from the volcanic bedrock below the chapel. Captain Brady would never have found this hidden passage had the old monk not kept looking at the floor below the altar. His pulsed raced as he directed his flashlight down the dark cavity. He told two of his men to come with him as he started down into the unknown.

The stairway continued down for approximately thirty feet and ended in a narrow passageway. The wall of the passage was dark and appeared to have been cut into strange patterns. He had seen some of these same carvings on the old Monastery by Lake Tana. He was soon to understand that this is the legendary twelfth or lost church, another of the below ground churches that had been carved out of the volcanic bedrock, like the ones he had seen earlier. The Chapel of St. Mary has been built over top of this ancient church. He now understood why only eleven of the legendary twelve churches had been found. Captain Brady could not help but notice that the stone floor of this passageway appeared as smooth as glass. It had been worn smooth by the centuries of wear by the bare feet of the monks coming to worship in this place. Moving along the passageway he soon came to an opening which led into a room about forty feet long by twenty feet wide. He could make out several furnishing and a long purple curtain at one end of the room. He knew instinctively that the Ark of God rested behind the curtain and call for the Priest to come down at once and look at what he had found.

When the priest entered the room they saw immediately that this room was arranged exactly like the temple that is described in the Old Testament.

This Temple contained all the furnishing and the curtain was set to conceal the most holy place, which is the place of rest for the Ark of God. They all became very quite and no one was eager to investigate behind the curtain. The voice of the old monk's warning, "Who can look upon the face of God?" was resounding in all their minds.

Captain Brady told the priest to check it out and again they began to sprinkle the blood that was taken from the ram sacrifice, on this altar and chant the prayers of old as they moved to the curtain. There appeared to be a mist or cloud in the air within the room but it began to dissipate as the priest moved behind the curtain. Everyone stood perfectly still and no one spoke until the priest backed out from behind the curtain.

"I can't tell you how I feel about what I've seen. I never in my wildest dreams ever thought anyone would ever again look upon this Ark of the Covenant. Before this Ark is where God spoke directly to Moses giving him instruction for Israel. It's here! It is here, "unguarded" in this strange place for all these centuries.

The Atang spoke, breaking the strange peace of the room, again in his same calm voice. There is no need for a guard. What human can guard God? God does not need humans to protect him. We need him to protect us. The old monk just stood calmly looking into the eyes of Captain Brady as if he were searching his soul. He spoke very softly, "Can you stand in the presence of God?" Captain Brady was speechless for a long minute before he regained control of his thoughts. Strangely he could not help but think of Rachel and he had a vision of her beauty for a few seconds.

Captain Brady then told his men to prepare the Ark for transport as quickly as possible and then sent a man outside to the alert the other members of the Unit that were still waiting outside the fence. Strangely the radios had stopped working ever since they found the Ark.

The member of the Unit waiting outside the compound were told to bring the cart to the opening in the fence, then unload and bring in the gifts of gold and the several other items of treasure that had been especially chosen for this purpose. These items were to be left as a gift to the people of Ethiopia as a reward for keeping and protecting the Ark of God all these many years.

The priests had opened the remaining packs that had been brought in to them. These packs contained a large animal skin and an even larger robe-like purple garment. With these items in hand the priests quickly moved behind the curtain. The animal skin was placed over the Ark of the Covenant and then the purple robe was placed over the animal skin. This was in accordance with the instructions given to ancient Israel whenever they moved the Ark. Once this was done, Captain Brady moved behind the curtain, there was the purple robe covering an object approx. four feet long and three feet wide, it was about 4' tall and it was evident something of an odd shape was at the top. He quickly understood the odd shapes were the two cherubs that made up the place of God and the cover over the Ark. This was where God communicated with Moses. On each side of the chest two long poles which were covered in gold extended from under the coverings. These poles were to be used by four men to carry the Ark.

The men assigned to carry the Ark quickly moved into place and grasp the poles. Captain Brady warned them to make sure they do not touch the chest. All the men present were aware of the story in the Old Testament of the man that touched the Ark to keep it from falling. He had been struck dead for he should not have placed his hand upon the Ark of God. As the men began to lift the Ark, the priest spoke loudly with the prayer of old, "May the enemies of Israel be scattered before them." It was no small matter to move the Ark due to the heavy weight of the Gold, which lined the chest inside and out, plus the solid gold of the cherub and cover, the stone tablets and other items that may be inside.

The gold used to line the Ark of God and make the cherub and cover was brought from Egypt when Israel escaped slavery. The men that made the Ark of the Covenant and cherub were some of the best craftsmen ever trained in Egypt. They, while working as slaves had crafted most of the beautiful art objects of ancient Egypt. It is believed that some of these same craftsmen may have made some of the treasure that was discovered in King Tut's tomb.

Once he moved away from the Ark, Captain Brady was able to use his radio again. He made contact with his men outside the chapel and told them to bring up the cart and make ready for them to leave the village. As the men carrying the Ark made their way outside, the old monk was given a injection that would cause him to sleep for several hours and allow the Unit the time needed to make their escape. The Ark was quickly carried out of the chapel compound on the shoulders of the chosen men. The old cart was quickly reloaded with their supplies and the Unit began its long escape route towards the Red Sea.

It would be a long fifty miles walk to reach the ship waiting to pick them up outside of the port of Adulis in the country of Eritrea. If it became necessary Captain Brady could summon a helicopter to transport the Ark, but doing this would draw unwanted attention and would not be according to the old method of transporting the Ark. It would be much better if they could quietly make this little walk, board the ship and simply sail home.

Resembling a band of nomads with their old robes again covering their uniforms, they left the village of Aksum as the sun began to rise. They were all stunned as they travel by Bieta Giyorgis, a massive monolith intricately carved in the shape of a cross and all forty feet of it below ground level. The scent of frankincense is very heavy in the air around all of the churches as the smoke billows from the many, crossed shaped windows.

They are moving very quickly now. It is very important to get out of the area before daylight arrives and the alarm is sounded. They will hide the Ark and rest during the coming day, and then travel mostly at night to conceal their cargo. It would be easier if the Ark could have been placed on the cart and then pulled along the road, but this is not the way the Ark of God is to be transported. According to the Old Testament it must be carried on the shoulders and lifted high for all the people to see. Captain Brady's instruction was to carefully follow all the instructions of old so as not to anger God.

As the sun rose and moved higher in the sky, the Unit made camp and concealed the Ark in a tent. Again the priest repeated the prayers that had always marked the transporting of the Ark. They would hold up in this camp until dark, and then make a fast dash to the border and out of this cursed country.

Chapter 12

Shortly after noon several barefoot worshipers passed by the campsite going to pray at one of the old churches. They will stand for hours resting on their prayer sticks and reading from their small worn prayer books much like the others they had seen along the way.

Everything appeared calm and tranquil as they rested from their night's adventure and scramble to put the village of Aksum behind them. They were very alert, waiting for the expected alarm and search for the people that had stolen the ancient relic and national treasure from the Chapel of St. Mary.

They were not accustomed to resting during the day and moving at night, but this is how they would travel from now on. It would not be wise to carry the Ark in open daylight with everyone in the country looking for it.

It would take them ten hours to reach the pickup point if they didn't run into trouble. They would then hide out during the day tomorrow and meet the ship and be picked up tomorrow night.

They must move slowly whenever they were around a village to keep from drawing attention. Once in the countryside Captain Brady would pick up the pace and move as quickly as the night, crude road, and heavy cargo would allow.

Everyone was restless as the day slowly passed. The whole Unit would become alert each time someone passed by on the road. Some of the men slept while others kept watch for trouble. They knew the alarm would have been sounded and everyone in the country would be searching the sacred relic. Could they make it out of the country without a fight? How could they fight a real battle with only non-lethal weapons? These questions were of constant concern for Captain Brady. He spent much of the day thinking about the strange feeling he had while in the Temple below the Chapel of St. Mary. The calmness of the old monk and his words of warning were haunting. Captain Brady knew he would have never found the hidden passageway had the old monk not given its location away by looking at the entrance below the altar. Could he have wanted them to find the Ark of the Covenant? And again his thoughts returned to Rachel and their future life together.

It was about three in the evening when the old Army jeep came down the road. The three soldiers were young and heavily armed. They stopped on the road and gave the Unit a quick look over, then started up and moved on down the rough road. Captain Brady could not believe the soldiers had not more closely investigated the Unit. They had to be looking for the people that had stolen the treasure from the old Temple under the Chapel of St Mary. He would remember to be watchful for the soldiers riding in the Jeep, as they would now be between him and the border.

As darkness began to fall the Unit broke camp and started their escape. After two hours of travel the road became extremely rough. Deep ruts caused the men carrying the Ark to stumble, and several times one of them would go to his knees. The cart dropped into one of these ruts and the wheel gave a loud crack as it splintered into several pieces.

Captain Brady knew he could not repair the cart, nor could he leave it on the road. He ordered his men to unload the cart and carry all the equipment off the road. The empty cart was pulled from the ditch and pushed a hundred yards off the road and covered with brush. He had his men dig a hole along side of a small hill and buried all of the equipment that would not be needed to travel. Each man kept possession of his weapons, even though they were loaded with rubber bullets and non-lethal ammo, and they kept their water and part of their food rations. To be in this desolate country without food or water would be suicide. The Ark of the Covenant was inspected, by the priest to make sure it was secure for the fast travel to come. Then the Unit moved out burdened lighter and at a much faster pace. They had to give the men carrying the Ark a few minutes rest every hour or so, as it was quite heavy, and they tired quickly from the poor footing on the rough road.

At a fork in the road Captain Brady could make out the tracks of the jeep going off to the west, away from the direction the Unit had to travel. Why had his luck been so good on this mission? Was there any way this luck would hold until he returned home? His gut feeling was that it would not.

All went well until they approached the border with Eritica. They had not expected to find guards on duty at this time of the morning, but there they were. It was too late for the Unit to avoid the guards, for they had already been seen. The Unit approached the guards as if they had no concerns. Captain Brady stepped forward and told the guards that they were worshipers returning from a pilgrimage to Aksum. The guards came closer and began to inspect the members of the Unit and the strange cargo they carried. As the two guards reached out and touched the coverings over the Ark, a single shot rang out, but both guards dropped dead. Captain Brady had fired once and both men had died. He could not understand, as he had not fired to kill, only to frighten. The shot sounded extremely loud and the single non-lethal shot should not have killed either man, but they both lay dead on the ground. The Unit did not have time to find out how this had happened. It had happened suddenly, and they must cover the bodies up quickly and move out before other guards came to investigate the shot.

The dead guards were quickly hidden in the brush and the Unit moved out very fast to put as much distance as possible between them and the dead guards. Captain Brady remembered his orders and warning that he was not to shed any human blood in acquiring the Ark. He hoped the orders and warning was that no "Ethiopian" blood should be shed. These guards were not Ethiopian and their deaths might not violate his orders, but it was too late to worry about that now.

They approached the port of Adulis just after daylight and found a deserted hut just off the coastline where they could rest and contact the ship. Inside the hut they removed the old robes and discarded all the remaining equipment except for their weapons. Now dressed in black uniforms, they took up positions around the hut in case unwanted guests happened to come their way.

From their hiding place and safety of the old hut they could see the activity on the roads and nearby village. They had heard the ambulance as it went to retrieve the bodies of the border guards and saw the police go in that direction to investigate. Everyone expected trouble and remained alert to every movement and sound.

Everyone was surprised at how easy the mission had been so far, and it was now only a short time until they would be safe on board the ship with their cargo. The blessing given them by the monk at the monastery by Lake Tana came back to memory as Captain Brady thought about the good luck they had experienced on this mission.

Once on the ship they could let down their guard and relax. This had been a long day waiting for night to come and the signal from the ship.

The signal came shortly after midnight and the order was given to make way to the beach and load the Ark of the Covenant into the waiting boat. The four men detailed to carry the cargo took their position, and as they lifted the Ark, the priest repeated the prayer again. Moving the Ark down the steep cliff to the shore was very difficult, but it all went well, and within an hour the Ark was safely on board and stored below deck.

They were on their way and everyone began to unwind as the coast faded into the night--- it had been a long hot walk to a successful mission. In a few days they would be back home and the Ark of God would once again be in possession of its rightful owners and home in Israel. One of the priests was heard to say,

"Glory returns to Israel, to God's chosen people. The curse will be lifted from our nation and Israel will once again be in God's favor."

Captain Brady sat outside on the deck smoking a cigar and looking up into the cool night sky. His thoughts were on the events of the last few days. He had expected the countryside to be covered with police looking for the Ark. He did not understand how the two border guards had died. The calm manner of the Atang was maybe the most disturbing of all. He mused upon The Question: "Could he look upon the face of God?" It's as if he had been expecting them to come for the Ark. He did not understand why they had not had more trouble and that strange feeling was still in his gut. What was he missing; could he not accept a successful mission?

Chapter 13

Back in Jerusalem, two men sitting on a park bench drew very little attention from those passing by. This was by no means a casual meeting. One of the two men was a spy and worked for whoever paid the most for information that he could gather. Presently he was working trying to figure out what was going on. He knew of the secret meetings in the Minster of Defense's office and that the Prime Minster had attended these meetings. He also knew Captain Brady had been training a group of specially chosen men for a mission, but this is where the trail was lost. There had been no further information for a week and the General was not happy. He wanted to know what the Jews were up to and he was willing to pay a huge sum to find out.

Habbe, a local mole, had gotten a bit of information about a man, an American, who had been picked up by the secret police at the library. He had seen the American going into the Prime Minster's office and had followed him back to the library. Habbe had watched him as he sat at the table in the back corner of the library. He was working with some old manuscripts and did not see Habbe. Habbe sat down at the end of the table with the American and pretended to be interested in the documents the American was reading. They soon became engaged in conversation. Habbe introduced himself as a Professor at the local university and extended his hand. The American stood and shuck hands saying, "I am Dr. Markus and I teach at the University of Mississippi at Oxford, Mississippi, in the Southern United States."

"What do you teach?" Habbe asked. Dr. Markus replied that he taught history at Ole Miss, but he spent his summers looking into a theory he had developed about the power of Biblical Israel. Habbe asked him to explain his theory.

Dr. Markus replied, "It deals with the power of Israel during the time the Jews escaped slavery until the destruction of the Temple Solomon built in Jerusalem. I can't go into detail about my theory just now, but I believe Israel will become a super power in the very near future." Habbe seemed interested in what Dr. Markus was saying but he did not press for additional information. He told Dr. Markus he had an appointment and had to leave, but he hoped to see him again.

Habbe could not get to a phone fast enough to call the General and set up a meeting to sell the information he had acquired.

They agreed to meet in the park and exchange money for information. Habbe could hardly control his excitement because he expected to get a large amount of money for this information. This time he would make enough money to pay his bills and maybe have a little left over.

The General was waiting on the park bench when Habbe arrived. He sat down and told the General about following the American from the Prime Minster's office to the library. He told him Dr. Markus was a Professor at the University of Mississippi and that he taught world history. He told him about Dr. Markus having a theory and that he expected Israel would soon become a super power.

The General asked, "How is this going to happen?"

Habbe told him he did not know and Dr. Markus would not tell him. He said the Jews believe Israel would soon become a great nation and would not fear anyone nor would they depend on the USA for their safety. They were expecting something big that would give them great power over all their enemies. Habbe thought the man knew more than he was willing to say, but he did not want to alarm him with a lot of questions.

"Is this all you can tell me about this Dr. Markus?" asked the General.

"That's it", replied Habbe, "Now give me my money.

"Sure thing," said the General, and he reached into this coat pocket, withdrew the gun, and fired three quick shots point blank into Habbe's chest.

The directive was given for all of Hamas' agents to find out what the Jews are doing and to find this man, Dr. Markus, that Habbe had talked with in the library. It did not take long before Dr. Markus was found, and after a little physical encouragement, the secret was revealed. Dr. Markus was not a strong man and the threat of personal injury was all it took for him to spill his guts and tell all he knew about the mission to Aksum and the Ark of the Covenant. Dr. Markus was given the choice of leaving the country on the next airplane or remaining in Israel forever. Dr. Markus understood what they were saying when they said "forever". He was on the next plane out of Israel and did not even return to his hotel for his baggage or care where the plane was going to land. He knew when he was in over his head, and dealing with the General's men was way more than he ever wanted. Besides he did not have a dog in this fight.

Upon getting this information, the General quickly made plans to intercept the ship carrying the Ark. This would be a great victory for his people. He did not believe the story this fellow Dr. Markus had told, but if the Jews believed it and he could take it away from them, well that would be victory in itself. If the good Dr. Markus was correct and this Ark did have some mystical powers and he kept the Jews from getting it that would be an even greater victory.

Chapter 14

The progress made by the Unit was confirmed two days later when the Ethiopian Government started making noise about one of their national treasures being stolen. Word was a group of military type black men had broken into the chapel of St Mary and made off with The Ark of God.

The men of the Unit had settled down on the ship and began to relax. Captain Brady could not help but feel something was wrong, but could not put his finger on the cause for his concern. His gut still told him danger was lurking about. He had heard on the ship's radio about the theft of a treasured relic from a chapel in Aksum. It had the Ethiopian Government all up in a stir. He was not too concerned about anyone discovering them or the cargo they carried now that they were at sea. He had wondered why it had taken two days for the alert to be sounded. He thought it was just the way things happened in this part of the world, where modern technology had not arrived.

As the ship carrying the Ark drew near to land, little attention was paid to the small fishing vessels sitting in the harbor. This was a huge mistake that was not realized until the first rocket hit the ship. The attack was fast and brutal coming from all sides at once. The attack ended quickly with the men of the Unit being taken captive. The men not killed in the attack were tied up hands and feet and questioned about the mission. Captain Brady was proud of his men as they all kept quiet and would not reveal any details, even when they were beaten nearly to death.

The General stepped in front of Captain Brady and told him one member of the Unit would be shot in the head each minute until he gave up the information on the mission and where the relic was hidden. The General then turned and shot the first man above the ear and let the blood spurt on the next man in line. He then cocked the gun, placed it to the next man's head, and looked at his watch. With only seconds to spare Captain Brady said, "OK, I'll tell you."

Captain Brady told the General everything he wanted to know, hoping to save his men. The General then sent his soldiers to locate the Ark that was stowed below. They returned shortly and told the General they had found the relic where Captain Brady had said it would be. The General then approached Captain Brady and asked if there were anything else he should tell him, the captain answered that he did not know anything else and had told him all he could.

The General smiled as he killed each of Captain Bray's men in cold blood. One after the other he shot them all, killing each one with a bullet hole in the head. He saved Captain Brady until last so he could witness as each of his men died. Turning to Captain Brady, the General asked, "Do you have any last words?"

Captain Brady said, "I was warned not to shed human blood."

The General looked puzzled by what Captain Brady had said, then smiling broadly he placed the gun to the captain's left temple and pulled the trigger.

With his last breath Captain Brady whispered, "Rachel, darling, I'm sorry."

The Ark was crated and moved to one of the fishing boats. Then the ship was set on fire and a hole blown in the hull. It was sent to the bottom of the sea with the bodies of Captain Brady, the other members of the Unit, and ship's crew.

Word did not reach Prime Minster Benjamin until late the next day, that the ship had sunk and that the Ark had been lost. There was very little information about how and why this had happened, only that the ship had sunk and it appeared there were no survivors as the bodies of some the Unit had been recovered. All of the recovered bodies were tied both hands and feet and had bullet holes in their heads. A feeling of great loss hit the prime minister as he received the news. He ordered his people to find out who was responsible for this and to find the Ark. It must be found and brought to Jerusalem, for he had convinced himself that the future of the nation was at stake.

The sunken ship was found on the bottom in about ninety feet of water. Divers were soon brought to the site and sent down to investigate. All that was found was more bodies with a bullet in the head and signs of battle on the ship. One body found was not one of the members of the Unit or crew. It was identified as a known member of Hamas. If Hamas had taken the Ark, what would they do with it? Would they destroy it? Did they know of its power? Whatever Hamas did with the Ark of the Covenant would not help Israel, for Israel had once again lost the Ark of God to their enemies.

Chapter 15

The Ark of the Covenant was quickly moved to Gaza and taken to the secret headquarters of the General. This is the appliance shop and secret room where the packages were assembled for the special deliveries going into Israel. Tonight the secret headquarters was a very busy place. Five packages were being prepared for tonight's special delivery missions into Israel's busy markets. The young heroes would be arriving soon to be fitted with their packages. The explosives were being prepared and the nails and screws were being positioned to do the most damage. The men preparing the packages were laughing and talking about what the Jewish newspapers would be saying tomorrow. This would be the night they would all remember forever. The plan was for all five deliveries to come ten minutes apart all in the same general area. They wanted to allow time for the rescue teams to arrive and the crowds to gather before the next blast would come. Then another and another and so on until all five packages were delivered. What a glorious night this was going to be. Allah Be Praised!

There was a knock at the door of the secret room and the five heroes were escorted into the room. They were getting younger with each delivery, and one of these was a cute girl about twelve years old. The heroes were nervous as they always were but tried to hide it like all those before them. It would not take long to wrap the packages around their waist and lock the devices in place. Each device was set with a tamper switch to set it off if someone tried to remove the package. The activation switch on these packages was a simple toggle switch, which the hero simply flipped when ready to make his delivery. It would not be long now before they would all be fitted and on their way.

Below the appliance shop and package- preparing room was a secret passageway cut into the bedrock fifty feet down to a hidden chamber. The General had selected five of his most trusted men and had them carry the Ark of the Covenant to this very secret place. These are the only men the General had allowed to know about the hidden chamber below the headquarters. They had entered the building through a back door and made their way down the passageway to the hidden chamber below. The Ark was set on a small table and then the General's men uncrated and removed the blue cloth and animal skins that still covered the Ark.

One of the men said, "I want to see what's in this thing." He grabbed the edge of the lid and began to slide it off. He moved his head over the opening and looked inside. He stepped back and stood shaking his head, unable to speak. The other men just looked at him and became uneasy seeing the look on his face. They all started to move away from the chest at the same time and entered the passageway leading to the building above.

Above the hidden chamber in the headquarters, the fitting of the packages was in the final stage. The last young boy was being fitted with the devices when something went terribly wrong. There was a huge explosion as all five bombs exploded at one time. Everyone in the building was killed and the ground shook as another explosion was felt coming from below the building as the passageway leading to the hidden under ground chamber caved in. All five of the men down there with the Ark were killed as the wall of the passageway fell on them. The Ark of the Covenant was now sealed in a void in the back of the hidden chamber that was buried fifty feet below ground. Every person involved in the moving and hiding of the Ark was killed in the explosion. The General was the only one alive that even knew the Ark of the Covenant was in Palestinian territory.

He was also the only one alive that knew about the chamber below the secret headquarters building and the ancient relic it now contained.

The next day's news story of the explosions that destroyed the large downtown building in Gaza and caused the death of several men, four young boys, and a twelve year old girl was written up in the papers, but not on the front page.

The news on the front page was that of the Palestinian leader, the General, being rushed to the hospital and being diagnosed with cancer. His cancer was of a very rare type which spread very quickly throughout the body, causing great pain; no treatment was known. Huge tumors developed almost over night and were growing very rapidly. The tumors would continue to grow until they burst the skin. This type of cancer had not been seen for thousands of years.

The General could not talk. Each time he opened his mouth, only a scream would come out. He was given drugs to kill the pain, but the pain was so great it would not let the medicine work. He could only suffer and scream in agony. The suffering went on both day and night for almost a week before one of his own men shot him in the head.

Within the next week there would be hundreds of cases of this same type of cancer in Palestine. Most of the Palestinian leadership and many of the members of

Hamas would fall to this ancient illness. It appeared nothing humanly possible could save Palestine; it was as if a curse had been placed on all of these people.

About this same time the most remarkable thing started to happen. It began to rain in parts of Ethiopia that had not seen any rain for hundreds of years. The countryside had started to turn green again. Flowers are blooming, crops are growing, and the rivers and streams are full for the first time that anyone can remember. Farmers are cultivating the soil and modern equipment is arriving to aid them in planting new crops.

The Ethiopian government has ended the civil war that had ravaged the country for over a hundred years. The killing has stopped and a new representative government is being formed with the help of the United States. Then to add to this good news, a deposit of oil has been found below the deserts of Ethiopia that will rival that of any in the world. It's as if a blanket of bad luck has been lift from this whole country.

There is an old monk in Aksum who looks out at the world and dances in the rains and watches as flowers bloom around the Chapel of St Mary's. He understands his burden has been lifted, his duty is completed, and he will soon stand before his Lord. The oath he and all the Keepers of the Ark before him had taken over the many years was to honor and protect the Ark of the Covenant until Israel came for it. He and all the Atangs before him had waited for this day to come, when they would be free of this awesome duty. He was now free to spend his remaining time on Earth watching his country come out from under the curse. He could not help thinking about how close the men came in not finding the Ark of God. If he had not helped them by looking at the hidden entrance they would not have located the passageway and his country would still be under the curse. This is why he had kept quiet and had not sounded the alarm for two days after the men had come in the night and had taken the Ark of God.

Prime Minster Benjamin sat at his desk and could only wonder about the Ark of the Covenant. Was it the real thing? What had happened aboard the ship? Where is the Ark now? Could the Ark have really restored Israel to its former greatness? Only God would know.

The only truly good thing he knew for sure was that the killing had stopped and it looked as if his country would have peace...at least for a little while.

He had been upset over the loss of the special Unit and Captain Brady. Captain Brady had been a good friend, his future son in law, and a good leader that would of had a bright future. The death of Captain Brady and the members of the Unit had been a blow to the Prime Minister. Who had killed them? How had they found out about the mission? Was there a spy in his Security Council? How would he ever be able to tell his daughter the man she loved would not be coming back to her? Would she ever forgive him for sending Captain Brady on this mission? He had promised her there would be no danger in this mission and Captain Brady would return soon. He knew the answer to his question. She would never forgive him.

Chapter 16

What had happened to Dr. Markus? He had disappeared. Had he returned to the USA and continued his teaching or was he also a victim? It was all such a mystery. How could such a simple plan go so very wrong?

At a secret location just outside of Washington, DC, a meeting is in progress. They are discussing the some of the same issues. Dr. Markus Friedman, or Special Agent Hayden as his friends know him, is talking to his boss, the director of the CIA.

"I am glad to get out of Israel in one piece," he said.

"Hayden, it looks like the plan worked even better than you expected. The curse has been lifted from our new friends in Ethiopia and has been placed on the Palestinians. The General is dead and the PLO leadership is in shambles," said the CIA Director.

"Don't forget about the vast oil reserves that our new friends have discovered," said Hayden. "This supply will force the prices worldwide to become lower and assure us a plentiful supply of cheap oil for many years to come."

"Yes, and Israel will continue looking to the USA for protection from its enemies," answered the Director. "We could not have allowed Israel to become too powerful. It would have upset the balance of power in the whole region and could have interrupted the flow of oil to the United States. It's better for them and for us if they continue to depend on the USA for their safety and protection. Yes, we can use the aid and protection we give them as a tool to control them.

Do we know what happened to the Ark, asked the CIA Director?

Special Agent Hayden was silent for a few long seconds, and then with a smile said, "I have a good idea where it is and I think it should stay right there for a very long time. It's better this way. Besides, who among us can look on the face of God?"

In Gasa an old building which once housed an appliance repair shop that was destroyed in an explosion is being torn down. A new mosque will soon cover the area and will offer hope and peace for the families in the neighborhood. But that story will wait for another time.

THE END!

Or is it?

FOOTNOTE AND DISCLAIMER

Within the pages of this book there are direct quotes from several commonly held books. These books include The Bible, Koran, and Torah. I have even taken some liberty to use some of these quotes out of context to help make this story more mysterious and interesting to the reader. I do not in any way want to imply that these quotes are my work or to claim the words of other as my own.

GLORY RETURNS
A STORY of FICTION
BY
<u>WAYNE REED</u>
Wayne Reed
wreed@watervalley.net

Made in the USA
Monee, IL
02 November 2023